P9-CZV-853

Hello, Reader!

Long ago and far away, there lived six blind men.
The blind men had heard of elephants.
But they had never met one.
"Let's go to the prince's palace,"
said one of the blind men.
"Then we can find out what the elephant
is really like."
So off they went.

To Mom, Linda,
and all the Golombiks
—K.B.

No part of this publication may be reproduced in whole or in part, or stored in a retrieval system, or transmitted in any form or by any means, electronic, mechanical, photocopying, recording, or otherwise, without written permission of the publisher. For information regarding permission, write to Scholastic Inc., 555 Broadway, New York, NY 10012

Text copyright © 1992 by Scholastic Inc.
Illustrations copyright © 1992 by Annie Mitra.
All rights reserved. Published by Scholastic Inc.
HELLO READER!, CARTWHEEL BOOKS and the
CARTWHEEL BOOKS logo are registered trademarks of Scholastic Inc.

Library of Congress Cataloging-in-Publication Data

Backstein, Karen.
    The blind men and the elephant / by Karen Backstein ; illustrated by Annie Mitra.
        p.   cm. — (Hello, reader!)
    "Level 3."
    Summary: A retelling of the fable from India about six blind men who each get a limited understanding of what an elephant is by feeling only one part of it.
    ISBN 0-590-90739-5
    [1. Fables.   2. Folklore—India.   3. Elephants—Folklore.]
    I. Mitra, Annie, ill. II. Title.   III. Series.
PZ8.2.B13B1   1992
398.21'0954 — dc20   91- 43076
                                                                    CIP
                                                                     AC

32 31 30 29 28   13 14/0

Printed in the U.S.A.   40
First Scholastic printing, November 1992

The Blind Men
and the
Elephant

Retold by Karen Backstein
Illustrated by Annie Mitra

SCHOLASTIC INC.
New York   Toronto   London   Auckland   Sydney

Long ago and far away,
there lived six blind men.
Although these men could not see,
they learned about the world
in many ways.

They could hear the music of the flute
with their ears.

They could feel the softness of silk
with their fingers.

They could smell the scent of food
cooking and taste its spicy flavor.

Together they took care of their home,
and they were very happy.

Then one day, the blind men heard some exciting news.
The prince had received a new elephant at his palace.

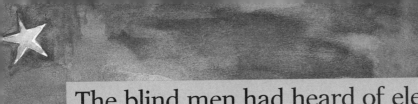

The blind men had heard of elephants,
but they had never met one.
They did not know what an
elephant was like.

"Let us go to the prince's palace,"
said one of the blind men.
"Then we can find out what
the elephant is really like."

Off they went.
It was a long walk to the palace.
The blind men grew hot and thirsty.

But they did not stop.
They could not wait to touch
the elephant.

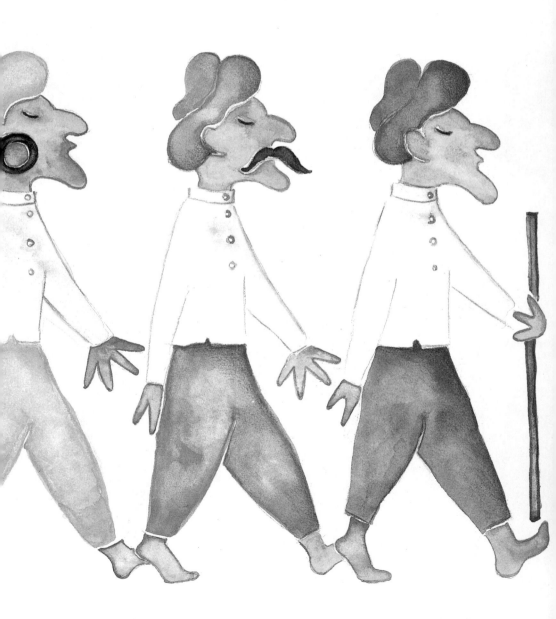

Finally they reached the palace.
A guard came to greet them.
The blind men told him why
they had come.

"Of course you may touch the elephant," said the guard.
"I am sure the prince will not mind."

The guard led the six men
to the animal, which stood quietly
in the garden.

The first blind man touched
the elephant's side.

"It is strong and wide," he thought.
"I think an elephant is like a wall."

The second blind man touched
the elephant's long, round trunk.
"Oh, it is just like a snake!"
he decided.

The third man grabbed the
elephant's smooth ivory tusk.
"Why, an elephant is as sharp
as a spear!"

The fourth man held
the elephant's leg.
He thought it was
as round and firm as a tree.

The fifth blind man held
the elephant's ear.
The ear was very, very big.
The elephant flapped it gently.
The fifth man laughed.
"It's just like a fan!"

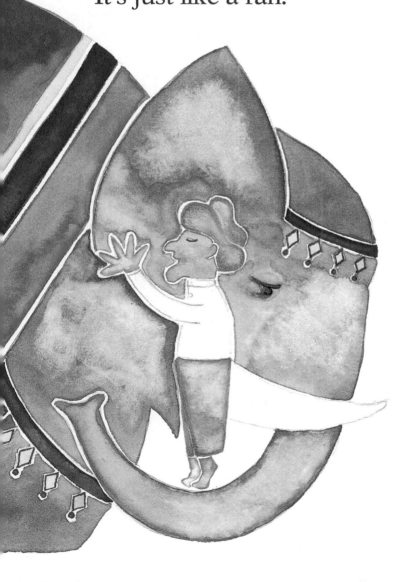

The sixth blind man touched
the animal's long, thin tail.
"An elephant is like a rope,"
he thought.

By now, it was midday.
The sun burned hot in the sky.

The guard took the six men
over to a tall, shady tree.
"Why don't you rest here?" he said.
"I will bring you some water."

While they waited, the six blind men talked about the elephant.

"No one told me that the elephant
is like a wall," said the first man.
"A wall?" said the second man.
"Oh, no. It is like a snake."

The third man shook his head.
"An elephant is clearly like a spear."
"What?" said the fourth man.
"An elephant is like a tree."

The fifth man started to shout.
"A wall? A snake? A spear? A tree?
You are all wrong. An elephant is
like a fan."

"No! It is like a rope!" yelled
the sixth blind man.

The sound of angry voices
filled the garden.

It was the sound of the six blind men
fighting about the elephant.

"A wall!" "A snake!" "A spear!"
"A tree!" "A fan!" "A rope!"

All the noise woke the prince.
He had been taking his midday nap.
"Quiet!" he called. "I am trying
to sleep!"

"We are sorry," said the first blind man.
"But we cannot agree on what
an elephant is like. We each touched
the same animal. But to each of
us the animal is completely different."

The prince spoke gently.
"The elephant is a very large animal.
Its side is like a wall.
Its trunk is like a snake.
Its tusks are like spears.
Its legs are like trees.
Its ears are like fans.
And its tail is like a rope.

"So you are all right.
But you are all wrong, too.
For each of you touched only
one part of the animal.

To know what an elephant is
really like, you must
put all those parts together."

The blind men thought about
the prince's words. They realized
that he was very wise.

"I will tell you something else about the elephant," said the prince. "It is very good to ride on. Now you will ride on it all the way home."

So they did.

And they all agreed that was
the best part of all.